C000256909

# Warm, Dark Pla

## By

## Mike Duke

# Acknowledgments

I would like to thank everyone who has been of immense help to me in this process. My wife puts up with me sitting in front of a computer for extended periods of time wearing headphones, listening to music, and not saying much of anything. (Hold on. Maybe *I'm* doing *her* a favor. Hmmmm.) Either way, I am grateful that she graciously supports all my writing efforts. Also, with this story, I had *numerous* friends who excitedly beta read this short novella and gave me their feedback – constructive criticism as well as praise. I can't thank all of you enough.

I felt good about *Warm, Dark Places are Best* at first, but I was still unsure about what others would think. All of you provided me with day after day of joy and confidence with one incredible response after another. I truly felt an incredible sense of accomplishment with each message I read from all my beta readers.

Lastly, a special thank you goes out to Lisa Lee Tone for editing this revised version for me and to Lisa Swearengin, Ta Bratcher, and Jason Morton, who are always Johnny on the spot ready to beta read my stories, answer numerous diagnostic questions that I usually have, or look at ALL the various stages of the cover design as it evolved and give their feedback. Thank you, everyone, sincerely.

Carl and Jessica walked into their new apartment, boxes in hand. They knew exactly what they were getting into.

Hell.

It was an absolute shithole, and most of the people who hung out in the hallways downstairs looked nastier than the cockroaches crawling all over the place.

As they crested the stairs onto the second floor, a gaggle of young boys was squatted side by side, pinning a roach to the wall before burning it to death with a lighter. Both Jessica and Carl stopped in their tracks and looked at each other, with a "What the fuck? " look on their faces.

Some old lady with a walker saw their concern and spoke.

"Oh, it's ok, y'all," she said, looking them in the eye, then stopped and patted one of the boys on the head. "Keep it up, fellas. You know what I say. Another one dead is one less crawling in your bed."

The lady cackled lightly and started walking again. As she approached Carl and Jessica, she greeted them with enough exuberance to create discomfort.

"Welcome to the jungle, newbies!" she exclaimed. "You'll get used to it, soon enough." The old lady extended her pale hand toward Jessica, first. It trembled and shook more violently the longer Jessica regarded it without taking it in her own hand. The lady's fingers were folded in at the root knuckles, a clear indicator her joints had been ravaged by rheumatoid arthritis. Liver spots covered the skin, and the veins were substantially visible.

"I'm Janet," she said, still waiting for Jessica to reciprocate her greeting.

"Been here the last 15 years."

Jessica finally snapped out of her haze and shifted the boxes to free up her right hand.

"I'm sorry!" she exclaimed. "Thank you. I'm Jessica and this is my husband, Carl. We're moving into 2C today."

Carl nodded and extended his hand after he sat down the stack of boxes he had been carrying.

"Pleased to meet you," Janet said and took Carl's hand as best she could.

"Nice to meet you, too," he responded politely, but not really feeling it. He had dreaded this day for weeks now and had made Jessica explicitly aware of his feelings just about every day since it was finalized.

Carl looked at the boys. They had burned one roach, skewered another with a large sewing needle or straight pin of sorts, and were fervently at work to set the new victim aflame. It seemed this was a favorite way for them to pass the time.

"Loads of fun and adult approved, as well!" the imaginary commercial for lighter and straight pin value packs targeting young boys flashed through Carl's mind, and he tried not to laugh.

Instead, he spoke to Janet. "Fifteen years, huh? Wow." He looked around, momentarily counting roaches on the walls, until his eyes lifted, and took in the ceiling. Then he *desperately* wanted to get in his apartment or back outside; either one, as long as it was ASAP.

*Anywhere, but this fucking hallway where those little radiation resistant germ-mobiles could fall in my hair at any moment*, he thought.

He released Janet's hand, abruptly, and turned to pick up the boxes in a hurry.

"I'm going to get these in the apartment, Jess. You two can keep talking."

He scurried away with a quick glance over his shoulder to see Jess launch a glaring look of ill intent in his direction. He noted it and calculated the penalty he would suffer later, but his hate for all things bugs was worse than any chastisement Jess might come up with. Instincts. Fight or flight. Hell, it was just good sense in Carl's book.

He pulled out the key, trying not to drop it as his adrenaline levels surged, and he fiddled with the lock like some teenage boy fumbling to get his zipper down for his first lay. Finally, it slid home and clicked as he turned it to the left.

Carl was struck by a distinct moment of relief before he rushed inside. The ceilings were clean. He expected more roaches he would need to exterminate immediately with the can of bug spray he had tossed in the box on top of his stack. To his surprise, though, there were no roaches. Not anywhere. He walked through the entire apartment, scanning every location he thought he might spot one, or the evidence of them, but there was nothing. Not one single sign.

"Whaddaya know?" he said aloud, to himself.

*Maybe management isn't as bad as they appeared. Must have set off a bug bomb and had the placed cleaned up good,* he thought.

Carl smiled as he put the boxes in their appropriate rooms and dug out a ball cap from one of them. Pulling it on firmly, he exited the apartment and practically sprinted by Jessica and Janet, who were still talking. He didn't say a word to either woman, much less dare to look Jessica in the eye.

He grabbed three more boxes and began the trek back to the apartment. At the top of the stairs, Carl felt his chest tighten slightly. His breathing became a little labored. Familiar feelings of shame gripped him, even though, as he looked around, the young boys were the only people in the hallway now. He shouldn't feel so self-conscious, but Carl had never been able to make peace with his disability since its onset.

He paused and took a moment for self-assessment. The tension in his chest wasn't full force, but his lungs were starting to complain.

*I don't have time for this bullshit today!* he silently yelled at his body and commanded it to move forward. Once inside the apartment, he reached in his pocket, retrieved the inhaler, and took a hit off it.

"Is your asthma already acting up?" Jessica asked. True concern filled her voice. As she looked at Carl and saw the beginning of an all too common episode, Jessica decided to shelve her developing plans of torture. She'd pay Carl back later for leaving her there alone with Janet.

"Yeah, a little, but I'll be all right. I'm not waiting for it to get worse." He pocketed the inhaler, smiled, and turned around to head back downstairs. In the hallway, a light bulb came on in his brain. He stopped at once.

"Hey, fellas." He addressed the four boys.

They all turned around and looked at him, a bit of disdain in their faces for distracting them from the scheduled executions.

"Would you guys be willing to help me for a few minutes?"

They looked at each other and back at him, a confused, blank stare on their faces that seemed to say, 'why would we?'

Carl wasn't the sharpest knife in the drawer, but he wasn't as dumb as he looked sometimes, either. He immediately discerned the answer he needed to give to their unspoken question.

"I'll give each of you a lighter …"

He paused to see if they would bite without offering anything else, but these lads were no amateurs. They knew one of the most crucial techniques in the art of haggling all too well.

Silence.

Carl knew he had to offer more.

"And I'll show all of you how to make a little flamethrower to really burn those cockroaches."

All eight eyes opened wide in unison, giddy interest painting their faces.

"But," Carl continued, "you'll have to catch them and take them outside to do it. Too dangerous inside the building."

The leader of their little pack spoke up for them.

"You need help bringing boxes up, dontcha?"

Carl smiled big. "You're a bright boy … ?"

"Derek," the lad said and stuck out his hand.

Carl took his hand and they shook.

"I'm Carl," he said.

"Well, Carl," Derek informed him, "you got a deal."

They gave a final pump to the deal-sealing handshake. Derek led the boys down the stairs ahead of Carl. They made short work of the contents of the truck - including bed, couch, and recliner with a little help from a man on the first floor who Carl promised to buy a beer for as payment. Jessica never had to carry another item in. Carl knew that would please her greatly, since she was always antsy to start putting things in their proper place right away whenever they moved.

When they were done, Carl walked across the street to the gas station and picked up a 5-pack of lighters and three beers, then returned. Derek and the boys were standing outside, patiently waiting for him to return.

"One of y'all go grab a thing of hairspray from your mom's bathroom," he said, walking up to them. "Make sure it's a metal can, aerosol, not the plastic pump hairspray containers."

Derek nodded and tapped one of the boys on the arm, who quickly bolted. In no time, he was back, panting a bit but can in hand.

"Alright …" Carl scanned the area and found a little nook where the walls dipped in a bit between buildings and had paved concrete instead of grass. "Come with me over here, out of sight," he motioned to Derek.

Carl squatted down, and the boys formed up in a semi-circle, intentionally blocking the common view of their activities with their bodies.

"OK. We did this all the time when I was a kid, screwing around. But you could definitely dispatch cockroaches like this." He smiled at them, but Derek was all business.

"So," Carl continued, "take your lighter and light it, and then get the hairspray ready." He turned off to the side and aimed it down at the concrete. When he depressed the button and released the compressed contents, the lighter ignited a spout of flame two feet long or more and scorched the concrete.

The boys all exclaimed their surprise and excitement.

"Holy fuck," Derek said, with a wicked gleam in his eyes. "That is awesome! Let me try."

Derek held out his hands, desperate to give it a shot. Carl handed the lighter and hairspray to him. He followed Carl's example and successfully made his own little flamethrower, then giggled with a glee that, it seemed to Carl, was not a typical experience for Derek.

"Here's something else cool you can do."

Carl held out his hand, took the items back, and proceeded to hose his left hand down with the hairspray, front and back, then set the can down. He picked up the lighter, flicked it, then lit his hand on fire, holding it up for all the boys to see. Their eyes got big. Carl gave them the old prom queen wave, twisting his hand back and forth with just a small amount of movement on the opposite plane to create that gentle wobble all the prom girls aimed for while riding by in homecoming parades. When it got hot a few seconds later, he shook his hand rapidly and the fire went out.

"That was soooo frackin' cool!" one of the boys shouted. He grabbed Carl's hand in his own and turned it back and forth, inspecting it closely for any burns.

"How did it not hurt you?" he implored, dying to know the answer.

"It's actually pretty simple. It burns the hairspray. When it's done with that, it will burn you too if you don't put it out. So, don't burn yourselves, or do anything stupid, like putting it in your hair or on your clothes. You'll turn into the Human Torch for real if you do. Capice?"

"Cool," the boy responded.

"Got it," Derek acknowledged.

"Alright, that's an extra. Y'all will owe me for that one, at some point."

Derek nodded and said, "No problem," then slapped another of the boys on the chest and issued a command.

"Ricky, go catch a few roaches in a jar and bring 'em down here so we can all have a go!"

Ricky nodded his head and took off.

"Alright, Derek. If anyone asks, I didn't show y'all how to do this. Right?" Carl looked them each in the eye.

"You bet. I'll tell 'em we learned it on YouTube. I'm sure it's on there, somewhere." Derek smiled big. "Thanks, Carl. You're cool in my book. If you need anything, let me know. K?"

Carl nodded his head and smiled, then said "you bet" before standing to walk away. He waved 'bye' and headed for the apartment, feeling more like the kid in that exchange than the adult for some reason.

*****

At the top of the stairs, Carl ran into Janet again. He almost let out an audible sigh, but caught himself, though he couldn't hide the labored breathing.

"What's a young man, like you breathing hard for after just one flight of stairs? Something wrong with you?"

*Old ladies*, Carl thought, *no sort of personal information is ever off limits.*

He decided to just let her have it instead of trying to shuck and jive and avoid telling the truth. She would certainly notice soon enough that he didn't work anywhere.

"Well, Janet, as a matter of fact, something *is* wrong with me. Has been for the last 12 years. Workplace accident. A somewhat caustic chemical gas got released, and I breathed it in. I've had very aggressive asthma ever since. I'm on disability."

"Well, at least you still look fit," she spat out, without any sense of propriety. "And you have a looker for a lady, you do. Sweet girl, that one. Count yourself lucky. We all, eventually, go through some sort of bodily hell if we live long enough. It's who's with you that makes the difference."

Carl smiled at the little pearl of wisdom offered in Janet's apparently typical candid fashion.

"Me, at my age, with hands like this," and Janet lifted both her deformed hands, "kind of hard to wipe me arse sometimes, but Bob's a loyal champ. In sickness and in health, and all that jazz. He's a keeper."

Carl's faced blanched white and he coughed reflexively like something had flown right in his lungs that he didn't want one bit of. Perhaps it was called TMI.

Either way, Janet just waved goodbye and started walking.

"See ya around, Carl," she said, a mischievous grin spreading across her face.

Carl coughed again.

*I swear,* he thought, *some old people do that kind of shit for pure entertainment, or just sheer spite - their little way of trampling the fair flowers of youth while they, themselves, slowly wither to death.*

*****

Jessica was hard at work unpacking and organizing things when Carl walked back in. His breathing seemed a bit heavy.

"You OK?"

Carl plopped down in the recliner, shaking his head from Janet's personal revelation in the hallway.

"I'm fine, honey. Just give me a few minutes to sit and catch my breath, and I'll help you put our stuff away."

"So, what did you give those boys for helping out?" Jessica called from the kitchen.

"A five pack of lighters."

Jessica stepped out in view of Carl and gave him the stare that said stop being a smartass.

"You lie," she said, bluntly.

Carl raised his right hand and placed the left over his heart.

"I swear to thee, dear lady, and the Lord above, I do not."

"You're horrible," she said and ducked back into the kitchen.

"What do you mean!" he protested. "Janet wants them to burn the roaches. And, besides, it was the predetermined agreement… along with me teaching them something."

Carl's volume trailed off with his last few words.

Jessica reappeared.

"*What* did you teach them, Carl?" Her posture and tone said this was Detective Jess he was now speaking to, but the look on her face said she was already prepared to be utterly appalled.

"Nothing major." Carl waved his hand like 'pish, nothing of note here, lady, just move along'.

"What?" she repeated, her teeth gritted together.

Carl exhaled and spat it out.

"I taught them how to burn the roaches with a lighter and a can of hairspray."

Jessica's mouth flew wide, and he could tell she had just been uncorked, but Carl quickly cut her off and stuck a cork back in her. He held up his finger and stood up.

"But, I told them they could *only* do it outside, on the concrete. And that I never showed them. Now, don't worry, that one kid, Derek, has got his act together. It'll be fine. Hell, I did it with my friends as a kid all the time. Now, leave me be on this one. You didn't have to carry a bunch of stuff. Be happy and congratulate my social engineering skills."

Carl smiled big, a smile of proportions which hadn't been seen on his face in some time, now. Jessica sighed.

"Don't sweat the small stuff, right?" she inquired in a rhetorical fashion, knowing it was one of his favorite things to remind her of.

"Now you're running on all eight cylinders."

Carl pulled a beer from the plastic bag he carried in, cracked it open, and smiled like a cat who had swallowed one canary and had another waiting in its back pocket. He tipped the beer in Jessica's direction, as if inviting her to acknowledge his win in this conversation, then pulled the other out and extended it towards her, like some Indian peace pipe.

Jessica didn't want to admit he was right. She never did, but she stepped forward and grabbed the beer, her actions saying what she chose not to say with words. It was an understanding they had, and Carl knew how to work it.

Jessica opened the beer and took a sip.

"Well, I know you've dreaded coming to this place," she said, "but inside here it's not too awfully bad, is it?"

Jessica looked at him closely as she asked the question, trying to assess what his thoughts were beneath the surface - where he either kept things hidden or, occasionally, dredged them up to throw out into the open for all to endure. There wasn't much in-between with Carl.

"Yeah," he admitted, "inside here isn't bad. But I fear it's the calm before the roach storm eventually arrives. There's no way they won't be in here at some point with how many are outside. On the other hand, as annoying as that lady, Janet, seems, she's nice. And the boys are cool. I think they may even look out for us a little after what I did for them. My biggest concern, besides the roaches getting in here, is the big human cockroaches around here. I saw a couple of hoodlums when I went across the street. They looked me up and down like a prospective piece of meat but didn't do anything. We're both going to have to take precautions when we are coming and going. It would be easy to become a statistic around here."

Jessica gave Carl an ingratiating smile, as she walked towards him and knelt in between his legs.

"They didn't want to mess with you, baby, because they could smell the tiger in you. They knew a predator when they saw one."

Carl let out a 'harrumph' sound spontaneously. The knowledge of what he was now compared to years gone by clearly hung heavy on his brow.

"I don't know about that. I feel more and more like an old man holding onto a weapon, scared he might have to use it 'cause he's too decrepit to do anything else."

He patted his right, front pocket to indicate the small, hammerless revolver he kept there at all times, his concealed carry permit always ready in his wallet, as well. It was a gift from his father several years ago when Carl was first injured and his life changed forever.

His dad understood what it meant for a man to lose his strength, his core vitality, and the ability to protect himself on his own, without looking to anyone or anything else for help. He had been in a bad motorcycle accident when Carl turned thirteen. His dad's left leg was never the same after that, and a cane was standard issue for the rest of his life.

Carl gazed off into the bedroom, not wanting to look Jessica in the eye. He hated feeling weak, much less acknowledging it to her.

"Hey," Jess tried to regain Carl's attention. "Remember that old saying? The one about being as good once as you ever were? You may not be able to train and spar like you used to do, but you can still be a badass if you need to be. You're still dangerous in my book; no doubt about it. So, chin up. I love you."

Carl stared deadpan at her.

"Did you just use some old redneck saying to give me life advice?"

Jessica giggled and took another sip of her beer.

"That I just did, good sir. Yes, I did. And, it's true." She took another sip. "And you know it," she said, tipping the beer in his direction, a subtle demand that he not argue with her on this one.

"Hmmm. Alright," Carl said, then downed his beer and smiled at Jessica. "Tell me, does that apply to certain *other* areas of performance as well, good lady?"

Jessica caught his drift but looked around the apartment. There was so much left to unpack, and the mattress and box springs were still leaned against a wall along with the bed frame.

"The bed's not set up yet," she said plainly. A hint of sadness edged her voice. The thought of not being able to take advantage of this uncommon spontaneity was depressing.

"Excuse me, dear lady, but your protests are insignificant in stature and easily remedied."

Carl stood, kicked off his shoes, and walked into the bedroom, where Jessica watched him lay the box springs on the floor then simply lay the mattress on top without worrying about setting up the frame. He walked back and extended his hand. Jessica took it and he helped her stand. Without warning, Carl scooped her over his shoulder and headed to the bedroom. Jessica squealed in delight, even as she kicked her feet and struggled in mock fashion.

"Methinks the lady protesteth falsely."

Carl tossed her down on the bed, unbuckled his pants, and stripped them off along with his underwear.

"What do you take me for, dear sir? A mere harlot?" Jessica laid her hand, dramatically, across her heart.

"Actually, no," Carl said. "The lady is the rightful spoils of my warfare conducted this very day in taking over this fortress, and I will have thee as my reward, whether thee agrees to it or not."

Carl squinted a provocative look, challenging Jessica to take the bait and run with it. It had been a long time since they had done this, but from the look on her face, Carl could tell she was down for the game.

"You, sir, will have to take it if thou really wanteth it. I will not go quietly." Jessica smiled, coyly, even as her eyes flashed a lustful desire for the delicious struggle that was about to begin.

Carl grabbed Jessica by her feet and pulled her to the edge of the bed, lifting her until her ass dangled in the air. He quickly wrapped his one arm around both legs to hold her there while he unbuttoned her pants with the other. Once the waist was loosened, he shook her up and down until they peeled off along with her underwear. She plopped back down on the bed, naked and exposed from the waist down, vulnerable to any attempts he would make to penetrate her.

Jessica shrimped her hips back and forth to make space between them, smiling the whole time, but still trying to play at being unwilling to a degree. As

Carl came forward on his knees, she used her feet to push his hips away. He snaked his arms inside and under her legs before she could maneuver them out of his grip. He lowered his head and locked both arms at the crook of her hips, pulling her in and burying his face in her groin.

A moan escaped Jessica's mouth as her back arched in delight. She let him devour her for a short time before she forced herself to keep the game afoot. She shifted her hips and pressed the back of one thigh down on his head, forcefully pushing him onto his side. She skittered back across the bed, her toned leg muscles rippling as she went. Jessica came to rest on her knees, body erect, head held high. She cast a challenging look down on Carl as she took off her shirt and bra and tossed them aside.

"You canst not have me, wretched sir. I am strong and can take care of myself, as you have now seen. I will resist thee to my dying breath." She shook her head in feigned defiance.

A devious smile sprang to Carl's mouth. He was giddy as a schoolboy.

"My lady, prepare to have your hindquarters chastised for this insolent struggle against your rightful master. Hah!"

Carl lunged forward, and they tied up arms, jockeying for position. Carl didn't use his size and strength to his advantage right away. It kept things sporting and more fun for them both. They both executed techniques they had learned in the earliest days of their relationship when they trained in Brazilian Jiu-Jitsu together. During that time, they both became skilled in how to wrestle and submit people with joint locks and chokes.

This had been their form of occasional play during sex years ago but had slowly disappeared over time after Carl's workplace accident.

Jessica loved the pursuit, the push and pull, the maneuvering for one end only. Their sheer desire on display. The way Carl struggled to have her aroused every inch of Jessica's skin and caused her to become unusually wet. She truly had missed this, the challenge, the roughhousing, but especially the way it made her feel so wanted.

Carl was now overcome with his desire for Jessica. He pressed forward with no thought as to what she might do. She seized the opportunity and hip tossed him across the bed. As he landed she slapped him full on in the face before withdrawing a couple of feet. Jessica's own face was ablaze with hormones and joy and a titillating cat-and-mouse adrenaline rush coursed through her whole body.

"You, sir, are over-confident and unworthy of my deliciously moist nether-victuals," she declared, trying desperately not to laugh. "A real man would not have made such an amateurish error."

Carl read her like a well-perused book, intimately familiar with each page, even if it had been some time since he observed these specific portions of text. Jessica longed for him to catch her, fair and square, to exert his dominance and conquer her. She knew he could. Every fiber of her body visibly quivered before him. She ached for him to do it *now*, without *any* further delay.

"You mistake coy restraint and playing with my food for the real predator's pounce, my lady. So be it! Thou hast asked for it with your lips and eyes and the heady scent of your sultry pheromones," he said, then spread his arms wide, and issued his declaration of licentious war with a deep, baritone voice that boomed within the bedroom.

"Prepare thee now to see this beast in all his devouring glory!"

Jessica laughed out loud as Carl moved forward. She reached out to wrestle with him again. Carl dropped low at the last second, his redirect allowing him to circumvent her defenses. He buried his cheek in her stomach, wrapped his right arm around her lower back. Hooking his fingers into her hip bone, he pulled and slipped around towards Jessica's back. Carl hooked under her left arm and cupped the back of her head with his left hand, right hand hugging her abdomen. Before Jessica could struggle, he forced her face toward the bed, reached between her legs to grab her free hand, and pulled, forcing her hips to meet his own. Jessica squealed in surprise, then moaned.

Jessica was ready for him. Carl slid inside her and she released a muffled scream of pure pleasure at having been caught at last. The game was over and now it was time to get down to business.

The sex was a fervent commotion of rapid shouts, moans, and squalls, escalating to a crescendo of howling chaos that surely gave Janet, the boys, and anyone else above or below them something to talk about concerning the newest tenants.

Breathing heavily, they collapsed and held each other for some time in silence, except for a few glowing compliments on each other's performances. In time, they nodded off for a nap then rose again an hour later to continue setting up their new home together, both feeling happy and quite content.

\*\*\*\*\*

Over the next few days, they managed to get everything put away. Neither of them left the apartment except to go buy a few groceries. Jessica filed her unemployment documents over their computer. She had tried applying to several places online. Fewer and fewer employers wanted someone to walk in and make face to face contact anymore, which just made it easier to be ignored and judged according to a few mere words on paper. Words, Jessica believed, could never fully represent who she was.

It was very frustrating, and the pressure was on. Her unemployment would be running out soon, and she didn't think they would qualify for welfare in addition to Carl's disability. But his disability wasn't enough to support them financially, and they both knew it.

He hadn't been able to work long enough to generate anything in Social Security. Carl had drawn the short straw at a very young age. Just having entered the workplace a couple of years prior, he was cutting his teeth on a shit job in a shit factory that didn't give a damn for their employees. Carl's father had managed to get him a job at the same chemical plant that he had worked at for some twenty-five years. It had been a good place to work, at first, but a year after Carl started, a group of investors bought out the company, and everything went to hell with great haste.

They forced people, like Carl's dad, into retirement with packages far less valuable than what they had been promised by the past owners. But there was no choice. Take it or leave with nothing – fired. A year later, the accident happened, and the company fought Carl tooth and nail. They tried to blame him and denied him any disability until the court finally ruled in his favor. Only thing though, the judge ordered just a fraction of what Carl's attorney was asking for. He couldn't help but think that there was some connection between the judge and the company; a favor owed, perhaps. Either way, it was a railroad dry fuck all around, and now Carl was financially and physically locked into an unchangeable set of circumstances that only got worse as the cost of living rose and his body aged. He was only thirty-five years old, but Jessica knew he felt like sixty half the time.

She hated it; hated what it did to him - especially what it did to him emotionally. It was like gangrene, rotting him from the inside out, but he couldn't die. Some days, it just manifested as a general malaise that zapped his sense of humanity, extracted all the color and smell out of life and turned it bland, drab, and meaningless. Other days, the anger would strike the boiling point and flash forward on anyone nearby. His tongue would flail madly, hurling venom like some spitting cobra, enraged.

But Jessica knew that was just the reality of it. Chronic pain and suffering do that to people, and the longer it goes on, the worse it is. Cycle down to crushing depression and despair and then cycle up to violent displays of hate and discontent with what life had dealt him. *That's just reality though*, she thought, *a vicious, inescapable circle.* But God forbid you were in its path when the bitter upswing took place and Carl's wrath flowed. At times, it had proven formidable indeed, though never physically directed at her. The walls, however, were a different story, and never completely safe.

Still, Jessica empathized and understood the struggle. Carl didn't just give in and let go. He fought the anger, the rage, and the disappointment that never stopped gnawing at his guts. He did his best to not let it reign. And like everyone, some days you fight your demons, and some days you curl up fetal, too tired to fight, and just hope they don't fuck everything up while you're gone.

Jessica surfed the ne, as her mind wandered, hunting for anywhere nearby that might be hiring. The only thing she could find was a temp agency. She dreaded the thought but saved the page. Sometimes, you must do things you hate for the ones you love.

"Adulting 101, but no fun," Jessica mumbled, to herself.

*On the bright side*, she thought, *five days here, and still no roaches have trespassed upon our aisle of bug-free tranquility. That has to count for something.*

She tried to be the 'glass half full' gal to offset Carl's 'this is damn near empty and it's not even decent beer, it tastes like piss' attitude.

The struggle was real.

*****

Carl was sleeping on his left side, facing the wall, when he stirred from a good sleep, something itching, or perhaps better described as prickling, across the skin of his right shoulder blade area. His brain swam into consciousness slowly, as if through a viscous fluid that struggled against him. But, finally, his lucidity surfaced and connected the dots, which revealed something on par with a paint by numbers picture in his mind.

He imagined it looked a lot like a big ass cockroach … and it was crawling across his shoulder, the sensations rising and falling in multiplicity with each light touch of exoskeleton legs as they traversed space in fractions of millimeters.

Instinctual reflexes, triggered by a fear common unto all men, engaged and Carl's left hand shot up to scoop at his shoulder, where he felt the unwanted contact. His fingers curled around the form and his hand flicked, the insect sent flying across the room to hit the wall.

"Fuck!" escaped his lips in a panicked cry.

Carl practically levitated into a seated position, as if his whole body uncoiled in opposition to the bed and propelled him upwards without ever using his arms at all, as they were already reaching for the switch on the bedside lamp.

Light flooded the space, dispelling darkness in a small circumference. It wasn't enough, though.

Jessica jerked into a semi-upright position, both hands planted in the mattress, her upper body twisted, hips and legs still left behind, frozen to the sheets.

"What's wrong?" she sputtered, her brain automatically wanting to understand just what had startled her awake in such rude fashion.

Carl ran around the bed, his cock shriveled with a primal fear as he scrambled to turn on the overhead light and find the offending pest. His hand stuttered back and forth, up and down, across the wall in search for a switch that his muscle memory had not yet had the hundreds of repetitions necessary to fully program his body to find in an instant.

His ears heard a 'click' that sounded like angels singing on high and the room flooded with a bright but soft white light.

Jessica stared at him like the madman he appeared to be. His eyes bulged as he skittered to and fro, frantically scanning every piece of carpet and along the edge of the walls.

"*What* in the hell is wrong, Carl?" she demanded in a firm voice, trying not to panic at the unknown, or give in to Carl's own expanding fear that seemed to be filling the room with each moment he did not answer her. She was convinced, then, that his fear was seeking to get inside her as well; to infect her.

"Do you know where the flashlight is?" he yelled at Jessica.

"Ummmm, yeah. I think so. *Why?*" She pleaded for an answer.

"Go get it! Now!" He spat the response as a strict order, and then followed up, knowing her well enough to be sure another question was coming before she did what he asked. "Just get it, Jessica! No more questions, not until that light is in my fucking hand!"

Jessica scrambled out of the bed and into the kitchen, where she tossed the contents of a catch-all drawer all about until she got her hand on the flashlight. She ran back to the bedroom, turning it on as she went. Carl had just finished picking up the couple of boxes that still hadn't been unpacked and tossing them on the bed to see beneath them. He snatched the flashlight from her grip without a word and threw the closet door open, shining the light every which way, moving shoes and other items around in a flurry. It was a desperate frenzy of activity to find the offending little creature of God so he could kill it … with extreme prejudice.

But as much as Carl hunted and searched, he could find nothing. No roaches, or anything else for that matter. He finally gave up and sat down on the edge of the bed. His chest tightened. He hurried over to the nightstand, grabbed the inhaler and sucked in deeply as he depressed the button.

He measured his breaths, nice and steady. The same. Each one the same.

INHALE for one, two, three, HOLD for one, two, three, and EXHALE for one, two, three. Over and over he repeated the cycle he had learned in training to help control adrenaline. Jessica gently scooted over behind him and rubbed his back with one hand and his hair with the other, waiting silently until he had things under control again. When he was ready to talk, he let out his usual indicatory big sigh.

Jessica calmly asked him "What were you looking for, baby?"

"Some fucking bug that was crawling on my shoulder and woke me up." He took a deep breath and let it out slowly.

"What kind?"

"I don't know. When I reached up and felt it, I just slung it across the room without thinking. Then I couldn't find it. But it was big."

Jessica continued to rub his back.

"You think the roaches finally arrived?" She gave a small, calculated laugh to try and set him more at ease.

"I don't think so. It didn't feel like a roach. It was long, three inches or more maybe … and narrow … and it felt like it had lots of legs. When I grabbed it, the little fucker curled into a ball almost as I threw him. What the hell does that sound like to you, Jess?"

Carl turned around to face her for the first time, genuine concern framing his face. She knew how much he hated bugs. Any kind of bug, just about. He didn't freak at just the sight of them, but if he thought they might get on him, that was a whole-nother circumstance. *DefCon* level ONE initiated. Jess thought about what he described.

"Well, if we were living out in the country, I'd probably say it sounds like a centipede, and a good-sized one at that, but I don't think you would find them here in the inner city."

More than a bit of terror filled Carl's eyes, as well as a powerful sense of incredulity.

"A centipede? A fucking centipede!? Are you fucking kidding me, Jess? Seriously, don't be fucking around with me about this…"

He tapered off and waited for her to speak again. She touched his arm, a soft, intentional connection meant to help him calm down.

"Yes. It really does sound like a centipede, but it could be something else. I tell you what. Let's sleep with the lights on the rest of the night. Most bugs don't want to come out in the light. They prefer the dark. Does that sound like a good plan? Hmm?"

Carl looked her in the eye and dropped his head, ashamed of his fear.

"Yeah. That sounds like a rational response, babe. Thanks."

Carl laid back and pulled the sheet up and turned on his side again, facing away from Jessica. Jessica laid back down as well and rubbed Carl's back until he could fall asleep. The rest of the night was, thankfully, uneventful.

*****

Carl used the daylight to prepare, in case it happened again. He put away everything in the boxes and cleared the floor. Around midday, he decided he needed a beer and went to the store to grab one, but only after shaking out his shoes vigorously. The flashlight was placed on his nightstand along with spare batteries in case the current ones failed during an emergency. He also designated a plastic lunch container to help trap the critter, because he couldn't just stomp it with no shoes on. But that made him think further, and he took a magazine, rolled it up tight, and wrapped it with some duct tape to keep it closed.

This, too, went on the nightstand.

It was like watching the kid in the movie Fright Night getting ready to fight the vampire in the final scene. At least that's what occurred to Jessica as she observed all Carl's preparations in silence, not saying a judgmental word to him at all.

*****

Carl slept through the night, not waking once until he began to stir from his slumber, ready to get up. He was lying on his back, his whole body heavy, as he came around in stages. Jessica was already out of bed. He smelled eggs … and pancakes. *She's such a doll*, he thought to himself, gratitude for her filling his heart.

The next sensation was not so pleasant. He turned his head to look at the clock and his right ear throbbed suddenly with pain. He rubbed the indentation behind that ear, trying to press in on the ear canal where it hurt.

Something pushed back … and then wriggled about inside his ear.

Carl's eyes went wide as he jumped out of bed, ignoring the pain, and ran into the kitchen screaming for Jessica.

"Jess! Jess! There's something in my ear! There's something in my ear! Oooooooooooo!! Fuck! Fuck! Fuck! There's something in my ear!!!" His voice was so high pitched and whiny, Jessica thought it could have been a kid.

"What are you saying, Carl? I can't understand anything but fuck and ear!"

He sat down at the computer, his right hand still pressed against the back of his ear.

"There is something … in my ear!" he spat out slower.

He used his left hand to hunt and peck and do a Google search for 'What does it feel like to have a centipede in your ear?' He hit enter and one of the first entries was about a Chinese man who woke up with a centipede in his ear.

Jess read over his shoulder and her hand flew to her mouth.

"Holy shit, Carl! You think you have a centipede in your ear?" Her stomach tilted a bit at the thought.

Carl ignored her as he read, all his focus on this poor man's tale and whatever similarities they might have. Carl's free hand covered his own mouth as he gasped.

"What is it!? What is it!?" Jessica was letting his panic contaminate her.

"I have the *exact* same symptoms he did. Woke up with pain in my ear and it feels like there's something wriggling in there! Fuck! Fuck! Fuck!"

Carl jumped to a standing position and began pacing.

"OOOOOOO GOD!!! What the *fuck* am I gonna do now? I've got a *motherfucking* centipede in my ear!!!" And again, as if he couldn't believe it himself, "I've got a *moth-er-fuck-ing* centipede in my ear, Jess!!!"

Carl's whole body trembled, and his knees nearly buckled. He turned in circles rubbing his ear. Jess quickly read the rest of the short article.

"They said the guy went to the hospital and a doc pulled it out with some forceps. We've got to take you to the ER. Get dressed."

"FUUUUUUUCK!!!" Carl shouted at the top of his lungs. "We can't afford it. We don't have any fucking insurance, yet! Is there anything you can do here?"

Carl whined as he asked for help, a trembling falsetto having overtaken his vocal cords. A tightness constricted his chest, as if a boa constrictor was wrapped tight around his torso, intent on killing him. He couldn't breathe.

"Hold on!" Jess exclaimed, as she pulled up YouTube and typed into the search bar. She quickly found what she was looking for to confirm her thoughts.

She heard the thump of Carl's body collapsing into the recliner and the ever too familiar wheezing noises. She didn't even look at him, just ran to the bedroom and returned with his inhaler, holding it to his mouth and administering the dose.

"Breathe, baby. Just calm down and breathe. It's going to be ok. Just breathe, slow and steady. Breathe. Alright, I want you to lay down on your side, that ear up." She pointed at his right ear, as she helped him lay the recliner back and eased him onto his left side.

"Alright, baby, just keep breathing while I grab something." She scampered into the bathroom, grabbed tweezers, then hurried into the kitchen to grab a cup of water and a dish towel. She returned, and moved about at a steady pace, implementing her plan. Jessica laid the dish towel around Carl's ear, set the tweezers down on his shoulder, pulled his earlobe out to open the ear canal, and started pouring water into it a little at a time.

Carl startled at the water entering his ear.

"What are you doing?" he questioned her actions, trusting Jessica, but wanting her to make it make sense to him.

"I saw a video, a while back, of a doctor getting a spider to crawl out of a kid's ear by pouring water in it until the spider had to climb out or drown. I looked it up, and sure enough, there was a video of someone doing the same thing for a centipede. Just lay still. It'll work and quick too, I bet."

Carl lay silent as Jessica poured more and more water in.

"I can feel it moving." Carl sounded like he was going to be sick.

"Fuck!" Jessica shouted, startled as the centipede came crawling out of Carl's ear in a hurry, speeding over his shoulder and dropping off the side of the recliner to the floor before she could hardly blink much less act.

"It's out! It's out!" she shouted to Carl.

"Where is it?" he shouted in response, not feeling able to breathe right quite yet nor sit up.

"I don't *knoooow*!" Jessica cried in frustration, as she stomped her feet and moved about in a tizzy, a deep distress at not knowing where the centipede had disappeared to seizing her.

After a long moment of silence, she screamed again.

"FUCK!!! I lost it! I lost the fucking thing, Carl! I'm so sorry!"

Carl blindly reached for her. He touched her side, and grabbed her shirt, pulling her toward him. He was measuring his breathing in between words.

"It's ok, baby. It's ok. You did great. You got the damn thing out of my head. That's the most important part. You're a champ. I love you."

Carl stopped talking at that point and focused on breathing to get the asthma attack under control.

Jessica grabbed the bottle of tequila in the cabinet, took two shots to calm her nerves then sat down to eat pancakes while she kept a close eye on Carl.

\*\*\*\*\*

That night the lights stayed on. Jessica had gone to the store to buy earplugs for them earlier in the day. They both said muffled goodnights after firmly placing the foamies in each ear. Jessica also wore underwear to bed, something Carl knew she hated with a passion. But she was concerned that if it could crawl in an ear it might be able to crawl up there, too. The mere mention caused her whole upper body to shudder in distaste and hostile aversion.

She got no argument from Carl. Hell, after hearing Jessica's fear, he put his underwear on too, afraid the centipede might bite his dick or crawl up his ass. They slid the little black eye blinders over their heads too, something else Jessica thought of, to help them sleep with the lights on.

Jessica rubbed Carl's back and tried to lighten the mood.

"Hey, love. Sleep tight ..." Her voice trailed off, as she paused.

"Don't you dare do it," Carl said, bluntly.

"Don't let the bed bugs bite!" Jessica blurted it out, busting out laughing as she did so.

Carl rolled over and started tickling her, his fingers scratching lightly all over her, trying to simulate a centipede's legs crawling over her flesh. Jessica's body twitched and turned and bucked and rolled.

"Stop it! Stop it!" she cried, with a limp authority Carl could never respect, but he stopped anyway, out of mercy and a desire to get to sleep and stop thinking about the heinous critter.

"You little shit," Jessica said deadpan and giggled a bit.

"You started it," Carl responded. "Just sayin'. Don't kick the hornet's nest, again."

He flashed a smile and rolled back over.

"Love you, babe." She draped an arm over his waist and drew close.

"Love you too, Jess."

*****

The next three nights passed uneventfully. Carl slept ok, but Jessica couldn't stay asleep for any longer than twenty minutes before waking up to look around. She did notice, both day and night, there still weren't any roaches in their apartment.

A search online revealed that centipedes eat roaches. But how many would there have to be to keep out all those roaches in an infested place like this building? That little thought did *not* help her sleep at all.

The fifth evening after removing the centipede from Carl's ear, they were sitting in the living room watching TV when Jessica saw Carl, out of the corner of her eye, jump out of the recliner and sprint into the kitchen. He started violently stomping the floor over and over, appearing to chase something across the floor as he missed, missed, missed and finally hit the target. He ground his foot back and forth several times before cautiously lifting it. There was a smear of innards on the linoleum, but the centipede carcass was embedded in the tread of his shoe.

"Gotcha! You little belly crawling fucker!!!" he yelled, in triumph.

Carl grabbed a napkin and pulled the centipede off his shoe, then presented it for Jessica to see that, he, the mighty hunter, had killed their deadly enemy. Once done with his display, Carl tossed its cursed carcass in the trash.

Jessica applauded him, energetically.

"Oh my God! Yes! I can finally sleep in peace tonight! This deserves a toast!"

Jessica retrieved the shot glasses and poured two shots, drank one of them, and refilled it, then toasted with Carl and downed the other.

"I'm taking a sleeping pill tonight," Jessica declared. "I do *not* want to wake up for nothing. I need some quality rest."

Jessica grabbed one out of the medicine cabinet, downed it and told Carl she was laying down, naked.

"Ooo la la!" Carl said, a little sarcastically, knowing there would be no sex after a sleeping pill. "I'll be right there."

In no time, they were both out cold, content, and feeling secure, even without the lights, ear plugs, and underwear.

*****

Carl was snatched from his blissful slumber by Jessica jumping up and down on the bed, making sounds like an alley cat squalling before a fight or sex, or both. He sat up and opened his eyes to see Jessica go from jumping to bent over, as her hips cringed backward and gyrated about in a way which was not the least bit sensual. Pain and hysteria had seized her. There could be only one possible explanation, it seemed to Carl and, at that moment, he had the strangest thought intrude upon his brain, amid this chaotic fervor.

*There is no possible combination of words that could possibly comfort a woman who believes a centipede is crawling around up inside her twat.*

"Nope. Not one," he told himself, out loud. "Unh, unh."

He stared on, in shock, unable to completely accept that this situation could, indeed, be happening. It seemed more likely to be a dream, but Jessica's next shriek hit such a high note it hurt Carl's ears.

The surreal quality of what was happening wore off, as if on cue, and his mental faculties began firing on all cylinders. Jessica had saved the day for him. He began thinking frantically, trying to determine what he could do to save her from this hell that could only be exponentially worse than the centipede being inside his ear.

*She has a centipede inside her vagina*, he thought again, and shivered at this terror that no sane person would ever want to even consider, much less give voice to. But it was happening, and Carl needed to man the fuck up and be the fucking hero, he told himself.

Jessica fell flat on the bed and began kicking, twisting, and bucking wildly. She was like some crazy woman in a possession movie where the priest is now waist deep in the exorcism rites, locked in mortal struggle with the demon, speaking in Latin, throwing holy water and gripping his crucifix as he presses it to the creature's forehead, causing the demon to make the girl's body go completely spastic. *That's exactly what my wife looks like, right now,* he thought, mind sliding back, briefly, into a dumb morass of inaction, overcome by these traumatic and bizarre events.

"Think, Carl. Think!" He slapped himself in the face, as he continued to speak out loud and help him keep moving forward. "Aaarrgghh! Think! Think! Think! What can you do? Ummmm … If she used water in my ear to make it want to leave, what the fuck can I use to do the same thing to her pussy?"

He looked around, unable to think of something constructive.

"Dammit, man! It's not like I've got a fucking garden hose lying around! What can I do!?"

Carl palmed his forehead, hard, and something suddenly clicked.

"A douche! A douche!" he exclaimed in utter excitement at a possible solution.

"Fuck! Jess! Where do you keep your pack of strawberry douches?" She didn't answer. In fact, she wasn't screaming anymore. Carl looked over. Jessica was unconscious, her body doing a little jig; a mild seizure perhaps.

Carl let loose a startled yelp but kept his composure. He ran to the bathroom and looked under the counter, tossing stuff out until he found the box of douches. He quickly read the directions and prepared two of them, just in case it took more water than he thought. Scrambling back into the bedroom, he inserted it into her vagina and began squeezing it in a steady manner, pushing the fluid up inside her.

When the first one was empty, he tossed it aside and picked up the other. He was getting ready to put it in and start round two when he saw dark-colored antennae protrude from his wife's vagina; something no man should ever have to imagine, much less watch.

He waited, unconsciously holding his breath at this weird, totally alien encounter, something that, possibly, had never happened before in the history of mankind, he thought. His stomach knotted as more of the antennae appeared, far too long, in fact, for the size of the centipede he had killed. What followed next was a series of glistening armored plates, a deep brownish-red in color. They covered the head and each segment of this gigantic centipede's body as it squeezed out, squirming back and forth to help free one set of legs at a time from Jessica's labia. Every limb fluttered lightly up and down, independent of one another, meticulously searching for any point of purchase to pull its body out by.

Carl felt light headed. The room was beginning to spin, the world flexing and relaxing with each breath he struggled to take in. The impossibility of what he was seeing overwhelmed his dire need to deny what his own eyes were telling him.

"Lying eyes! Lying eyes!" he muttered loudly to himself, closing them hard, and rubbing them vigorously, before opening them again, only to have the traitorous bastards reveal the inconceivable truth. Reality had become one long, insane moment, drawn out like some man dropping from the gallows in slow motion, waiting for the noose to snap tight and end it all.

The inexorable dread of that moment was nearly unbearable. It was not only elongated, but exponentially more insidious than any execution or torture he could fathom.

As he looked on, Carl realized that about seven inches of the giant centipede's body was exposed now. It continued to flail back and forth, seeking freedom. A pale white belly peeked out here and there, even as the large overlapping plates that covered each segment of its back flexed side to side and open and closed. It used the multi-jointed yellow and red legs to pull against both Jessica's inner thighs and the comforter.

Carl could take it no longer. His lungs closed tight, and the wheezing began.

The giant centipede secured sufficient traction as its legs hooked into the covers and pulled with an incredible strength, allowing it to rapidly extract the rest of itself from Jessica's flooded vaginal canal.

Life resumed normal speed for Carl as another six inches or more quickly appeared before the centipede plopped out onto the bed, dual horn-like objects protruding from its rear shaking at the ceiling in a flurry as it took off in an unpredictably snaking path. Before Carl could react, it disappeared over the edge of the bed and was out of sight.

Jessica's seizures stopped about the same time Carl passed out from lack of oxygen.

\*\*\*\*\*

Jessica came to with a gasp, sitting up and covering her groin with both hands, the instinct to protect her currently most vulnerable and sensitive area kicking in with consciousness.

The first thing she noticed was that it didn't hurt inside anymore. Not bad anyway. Just a dull ache, like the fading memory of something quite painful. Though, the outside of her lips and inner thighs felt uncomfortably pricked, as if by small thorns. The second thing she saw was Carl passed out in front of her ... and she couldn't tell whether he was breathing or not.

She immediately located his inhaler, stuck it in his mouth, and squeezed it, then pinched his nose, tilted his head back, and blew into his mouth to try and make sure the medicine got to his lungs. After a couple of breaths, Jessica listened to his chest. She could hear the heart doing its job, thump, thumping along. He was breathing too, just ultra-shallow.

After a minute of intense inspection, Carl coughed hard, and his inhalations became normal again, if somewhat labored.

Jessica let out a huge sigh. This wasn't the first time it had happened. She'd had to force the medicine into his lungs while he was unconscious a handful of times over the last 12 years of their marriage, but it always freaked her out.

She looked around, trying to figure out what had happened. She observed a large wet spot where her hips had been when she passed out. There was a very narrow, light trail of water snaking across the covers and off the bed. She suspected that might have been a centipede running off … but to make that wide of a trail, it would have been huge. Upon scanning the room further, she saw a full douche laying on the bed and an empty one on the floor.

She looked at Carl with nothing but love, her face softening as she considered what he must have gone through, seeing her pass out, and then having to use a douche on her and watch a centipede crawl out of the place that he always craved to be inside himself.

He had surely scrambled to come up with a way to get it out of her while working himself up into a panic, eventually passing out when the asthma attack put his lungs on full lockdown.

Jessica felt closer to him right then than she had in some time. Lying down, she curled up against Carl and rubbed his chest lightly until he finally woke up.

*****

"I swear to God, Jess! I am *not* messing with you! That thing was as long as my fucking forearm and a good inch and a half or more in width! I'm fucking scarred for life after watching that thing crawl out of your cooch. All squirming and flailing around."

Carl sat forward in the recliner as he made twisting and flopping movements with his hands and arms to illustrate what he meant. It clearly grossed Jessica out by the contortions her face went through.

Carl didn't want her to possibly puke, so he decided to pursue a little humor to break the granite level tension.

"I'm telling you, it was having to struggle damn hard to defeat the suction power you got there."

Carl pointed at her crotch to further indicate the location meant by 'there'. A smile began to creep across his face as he tried not to laugh at his own joke. Jess stared back at him, flashing her death-beam gaze at him. She was extremely flustered by the timing of his off-color humor, but the more he smiled and giggled the closer she visibly came to laugh with him. Carl held his grin and let it ride, hoping she'd crack.

After a long silence, Jessica was unable to hold back laughter any longer. A snicker escaped, followed by a short burst of giggles once the seal was broken. She slapped Carl on the arm, but never stopped smiling the whole time.

"The suction power of my vagina, huh?" Jessica tried to ask with a straight face.

"Your wonderfully soft and magical vagina," Carl corrected her, index finger held up to emphasize he was emphasizing a very crucial point. Jessica's eyes sparkled, and her mouth made an 'O'.

"Get outta here!" She waved him off with both hands.

The shit-eating grin spreading across Carl's face beamed brightly enough it caused Jessica to laugh so hard, she snorted. Carl cackled in response, and Jessica snorted again. They both busted out in unrestrained hilarity for some time, unable to stop themselves, tears rolling down their cheeks and ribs hurting.

By the time they settled back down, Jessica appeared quite relaxed, as if a load of tension had been released inside her body, all the way down to her toes and fingertips.

"I just can't believe the *size* of the centipede you're describing," she said, out of the blue. "I mean, I've heard of it; just not around here, though. You know?"

"I've never heard of it at all, but I felt like I was in that King Kong movie, with Jack Black, for a minute; watching Andy Serkis get eaten by that giant nightmare creature that should not be named."

The grin began to blossom again.

"Knock it off."

Jessica put the smack-down on any further silliness. Carl knew that look. It was time to do business and figure out just what the hell was going on.

"OK," Carl frowned slightly and adopted a serious tone. "How do you feel …
down there? And by the way, have you ever had seizures before? Because you
sure as hell looked like you were having one when you passed out."

Jessica looked surprised at the mention of seizures.

"Well, down there feels ok, right now. No more serious pain and no more
squirmy wiggles, just a little bit of soreness and some prick marks on the outside.
As far as seizures, my mom used to get grand mal seizures every now and then. I
had one when I was a teenager after having a panic attack."

"Alright. That explains that, pretty much, I think. I don't feel so worried now.
You *seem* fine." He let his voice trail off with an interrogative tone, waiting for
Jessica to confirm his assessment.

Jessica nodded her head.

"I do feel fine. A little fatigued, but that's common after a seizure. No biggie.
My mom rode 'em out like a champ all the time. No doctor needed."

Carl gave her a look of pure skepticism.

"What!?" she challenged. "I'm fine, and I'm not going to needlessly burden
us with any medical debt that can be avoided."

"And you're sure your little girl there is unharmed?"

Carl winked at Jessica, a mischievous look mixed with true concern.

"I mean, you know I've invested a lot in that product." Carl placed a hand over his heart to show his sincerity and commitment. "I can't be having it ruined.

Though I don't think I'll be able to touch it till after your next period when you've shed all those corrupted skin cells. I mean, *just the thought* right now is kind of turning my stomach a little."

Carl faked a burp.

"Oh yeah. That was, uh … chunky."

Jessica picked up a couch pillow and threw it at Carl's head. His arms flinched upward just in time to cover his face.

"You little shit! Knock it off," she said, pointing her slender index finger at his face as if she wished it was stabbing him.

She stormed over to the computer and sat down, but he saw the glimpse of a smile tugging at the corner of her mouth as she turned away.

Jessica spun around for one last parting shot.

"And, I'll have you know, the douche you used in me was perfectly capable of cleaning me out … but I *am* going to shower as soon as I look something up."

She faced the computer again, and her fingers began rattling away on the keys. It didn't take long before Carl heard her sharply suck in wind. He looked up to see both Jessica's hands covering her mouth.

"OH, MY FUCKING GAWD," she said loudly, then started waving frantically for Carl to come over to the computer. "You have *GOT* to see this Carl!"

Carl quickly walked up behind Jessica, bending over her shoulder to get a good look at the screen. Jessica clicked 'Play' and everything went in motion. Some guy was holding up a giant centipede just like the one Carl had seen crawl out of Jessica. It was easily a foot long. Probably a little longer.

"*Scolopendra gigantea*," Carl repeated what he heard the guy say on the video.

"*That's* what you saw crawl out of me?!? It was *that* big!?" Jessica twisted her head around and looked at Carl with absolute incredulity.

"Honey, *that* is exactly what I saw crawl out of you." Carl tapped the screen for emphasis.

Jessica looked back at the monitor and just stared at it in awe. A shiver ran up her spine, causing her whole body to shudder briefly.

"Fuck me," Jessica said plainly, wiping her hands down her face. "This is just too fucking crazy. It says here these are native to South America and the Caribbean. But there's other places that have similar types that are just as big or bigger: Vietnam, Texas and some other desert states, as well as Hawaii."

Jessica paused for a long moment then more mumbled to herself than Carl, "What the fuck are they doing in our apartment?"

\*\*\*\*\*

That night, at bedtime, the lights were on, earplugs were in, and Jessica had even dug out some old cough masks like they issued people to wear in ER waiting rooms when they were infectious. Those were strapped in place, covering both their mouths and noses. Jessica was freshly showered for the third time that day, her genitals thoroughly scoured with soap and a tampon soaked with more of the douche liquid inserted inside to both help further sanitize her lady parts overnight and make damn sure *nothing* could possibly crawl inside her. Underwear was added for additional shielding.

It took an hour or more, but they fell asleep.

Sometime later, it was a pulling sensation on her underwear that brought Jessica out of her slumber. She was fetal and facing Carl when a sensation of insect legs registered on the back of her upper thighs. It was accompanied by a distinct pulling at her underwear directly over her vaginal entrance. Every one of her muscles contracted in some instinctive acrobatic maneuver that sent her body spinning towards her side of the bed, completely lifted above the mattress. She landed like a cat on all fours and immediately saw the scolopendra.

*God, this can't be happening*, her mind told her, but she knew it was. It started to scramble towards the edge of the bed, but Jessica's brain was in the fight now. She grabbed the blanket with both hands spread apart, lifted it, then slammed the material down over the giant insect's body. Without hesitating, Jessica tracked her hands inward until she isolated the centipede and trapped it with the covers in a very small space. The outline of its twisting and turning form was clearly visible.

Carl's hand appeared out of nowhere. He had launched into action just behind Jessica, grabbing a pocket knife and opening it while Jessica did her part. He pressed the blade down roughly across the hidden form until he heard, and felt, the exoskeleton cracking, then he dragged the edge across it, maintaining a strong downward force. The blanket opened like a zipper as he felt the knife cut fully through the centipede's body.

He pulled the blade back and looked at it. There was a deep brown viscous smear on each side of it. He and Jess could both see the divided body parts spastically twitching and thrashing around through the slit in the cover, but it wasn't enough for Jessica. She pulled the blanket back all the way to see clearly.

It was cut into three pieces. The blade sliced through it while it was partially curled up. Carl scanned the body until he found the segment with the large pincers, then immediately brought the edge down; bisecting it just below the chitinous plate protecting the centipede's head. The pieces continued moving for some time despite the vivisection and decapitation.

Carl retrieved a gallon size Ziploc bag. After putting all the segments inside, he sealed it and threw it down on the bed, frustration evident despite their victory.

"Tomorrow, I'm gonna ask Derek and his friends about this freakin' monster." He pointed at the bag. "As much as they roam this place, I can't believe they haven't at least seen one of these around the complex at some point or heard rumor of some sighting. *And,* I'm going to call our piece of shit landlord and demand he hire an exterminator. Fuck this shit!"

*****

"What the *fuck* do you mean you '*can't* hire an exterminator'? I've got the corpse of a friggin' giant centipede in a *motherfucking* gallon-size Ziploc baggie … You think I'm exaggerating? I'm holding it in my god damn hand!!!"

Jessica stared at Carl, as he paused again to listen to the response of the landlord on the other end; all the while pacing like a caged animal, ready to attack anything that came near him. His neck muscles were rigid with rage. She hadn't seen him this pissed off in a very long time, but she knew his anger at life, in general, had been simmering for years, now. This was undeniably a righteous cause for him to vent some of that pent-up hostility and frustration that he had been fighting to restrain for so long.

Carl's whole body stopped all movement at once, right before words exploded from his mouth, the rest of his torso and head shaking like volcanic earth as the top is blown away in a pyroclastic cloud of destruction.

"*WHAAAAAAAT*!?" Carl yelled, holding the phone out in front of his face, to fully scream in it - his tone of voice ratcheted up several octaves, his face beet red. "I tell you what then, you *fucking* prick: if another one of these giant bastards shows up and hurts my wife I'll be on your doorstep faster than you can call the police, and I *will* fuck you up!! And, as an additional bonus, you piece of shit, I'll bring the cocksucker over there, and let him crawl down your *motherfucking* throat!!"

Carl threw the cordless phone across the room into the couch cushions and screamed, head arched back.

"FUUUUUCCKKKK!!! That mother-fucking bastard said it wasn't his responsibility! Can you believe that bullshit, Jess?"

He turned to her, livid with frustration. Jessica could tell he just needed her to acknowledge his right to feel this way.

"It's ok, honey." Jessica stood and walked over to him, slipping her arms around his waist from behind him. "You tried. And you're right. He's a piece of shit landlord running a piece of shit apartment complex. We'll handle things ourselves. OK? We'll make it work. It's ok."

She rubbed his stomach and chest lightly, rhythmically, as she spoke. In a minute, his body began to relax, the tremors subsiding until he was still. She felt him breathe in deep, chest expanding, then blow it all out at a slow, measured rate.

"How 'bout you go talk with Derek and the boys and see what they know? I think that's a solid starting point."

Carl turned around, and kissed her on the forehead, before giving her a long hug.

"You got it, Jess. I love you. I'll be back in a little bit."

Jessica kissed him on the lips once, and he walked out the door, the Ziploc bag in hand.

*****

Carl didn't have to search far, at all. Derek and the boys were outside, burning cockroaches with their homemade flamethrowers.

"Hi fellas."

Derek and the boys turned simultaneously to look at him, all of them looking guilty, except for Derek. Derek had the poker face, no emotion and nothing to indicate his activities. He might have been helping an old lady across the street or bagging dope or burning roaches with lighters and hairspray. You'd never know to look at him in that moment.

Derek gave a slight nod, in greeting, and Carl continued walking over.

"Hey, Derek. Guys." Carl nodded at Derek and then the other boys. "I need y'all's opinion on something."

Derek cocked an eyebrow, an unconscious show of interest.

"I need to know if you've seen something around the apartment complex, and if so, what you know about them. It's pretty gnarly."

Carl held out the gallon baggy with the giant centipede pieces inside.

All the boys perked up with recognition at the sight of it but waited for Derek to speak first.

"Did you find that in your apartment?" Derek inquired, cool as a cucumber. The boy was a natural at bargaining, Carl thought.

"Yes, I did Derek. And it was quite the fucking surprise, I'll tell ya. And ..." Carl caught himself getting angry again and paused, trying to reduce the emotions he visibly expressed. It would only make him appear more desperate and Derek would be keen to capitalize on that during whatever negotiations were about to begin.

"And the landlord says he won't pay to have an exterminator come out to our apartment. So, Derek, I can tell you all know what this is, and it appears you know something pertinent to my current situation. What can you tell me?"

"Well, first, is this you calling in the debt for the bonus stuff you showed us, or are we going to negotiate here? 'Cause I just happen to know some important things that you don't … about your apartment …"

Derek let that last piece of info just hang in the air.

"Derek," Carl said, a big smile plastered across his face, "I thought we were friends …" Carl placed his free hand over his heart as if the thought of them not being friends pained him.

"Well, Carl, we're friendly. This is true. Which also means we can help each other out. How 'bout that?"

Carl looked down at the Mafioso-style kid and smirked.

"Alright. So how can I help you out, after you help me out?" Derek answered.

"Another pack of lighters and four cans of hairspray."

"Deal," Carl said, without hesitation.

"Alright then," Derek grabbed the gallon baggy from Carl's hand and held it up. "This, here, is Scolopendra Gigantae. Native to Peru and other parts of South America, particularly within the Amazon Jungle. Now, as to how this big, nasty fucker ended up in your apartment, that requires a little history lesson." Derek gave a grin; the kind people give when they know something really juicy the other party has no clue about.

"They didn't tell you the last person in your apartment died, did they?"

"What?" Carl's mouth dropped open as the single word toppled out.

"Yeah. Actually, killed," Derek clarified, "but, ultimately, that's not important to your current dilemma. Anyway, the victim, slash tenant, was this middle-aged Asian guy who went by the name of Kenneth Wong. Weird, nerdy type and a real recluse. Hardly ever came out of the apartment. Did everything online; even had his groceries delivered. And if he needed something in a hurry, he'd pay one of us to go get it for him."

Derek indicated himself and the boys.

"Now, one day, after I went and got a couple items from the hardware store for him, he let me come inside, and *ho-ly* shit, man!" Derek's face became more expressive than Carl had seen it so far. "That crazy dude had about twenty fish tanks. All of them had one of these giant centipedes inside! Several of them were momma centipedes along with a shit ton of kids in various stages of development. Some looked like newborns, and others like decent-sized regular centipedes. If you didn't know what they were, you wouldn't realize they had a lot of growing to do. It was sick, though, man! I mean, cool and interesting, but nasty as hell at the same time. He was breeding them to sell. He was the supplier for some online store that sold lots of exotic insects to people for pets."

Carl felt a bit of nausea tickling at the bottom of his stomach.

"Anyway," Derek continued, "he must have started doing business with some shady, black market types and screwed someone over, cause two tatted up Asian guys showed up here late one night and shot his ass dead. I don't think even the police know how it went down, exactly, but I was down the hallway, just come out of Ricky's place, when I saw them go in Mr. Wong's apartment. They looked sketchy as fuck, so I went down there and listened outside the door. I heard talking, not sure whether it was Chinese, Korean, or Japanese. I don't know, but I think they were going to take all his centipedes as payment for something, and not just kill him."

"What made you think that?" Carl asked.

"Well, I heard Mr. Wong scream at them, and then the fish tanks started shattering on the floor. One after another, after another. Then it sounded like they were wrestling around, and more tanks got knocked over. One of the guys screamed, and then there were two muffled shots from a handgun. Maybe a silencer, I think. I scrambled down the hall and ducked into the edge of the stairwell. Right then, Mrs. Janet peeked out her door, holding onto her walker with one hand and her phone pressed to her ear in the other. She was talking to the police. Those guys busted out of Mr. Wong's door in a hurry. One of them was holding his neck and clinching a big bag in the other hand. The other guy was holding a bag as well as a pistol. The barrel was long and he quickly shoved it in Mrs. Janet's face, and told her 'Bitch! You ain't seen a thing!' and then took off."

"Wow. Holy shit. What happened next?" Carl asked.

"Well, before the police could get there, I peeked inside. Mr. Wong was stumbling around, knocking over the rest of the fish tanks. Freeing all the centipedes that the guys hadn't snatched up. After he finished crashing the last one, he collapsed and stopped breathing. I watched all those ugly bastards crawl off out of sight, the momma ones carrying their little babies, as they went. By the time the police got there, all they found were empty tanks. They never figured out what was in them before they left or when they came back around later, asking questions. I didn't tell 'em shit."

"Holy fuck," Carl spat out, in disgust. "You mean, there's a shitload of those monsters in my apartment, Derek?"

"Well, maybe. Hard to say where they went. Whether they all stayed in your place or went somewhere else. I mean, they like warm, dark places best …"

Derek paused for a moment and then exclaimed "Oh shit!", an epiphany having struck him, suddenly.

"What!?" Carl demanded.

"One of the big water heaters for the complex is in between your apartment and the old man next to you, the one closest to the stairs. I bet those fuckers are in your walls, all around that water heater, cozy as hell."

"You know something strange?" Carl asked Derek.

"What?" Derek was genuinely interested in what Carl might have to say.

"We haven't seen any roaches in our apartment since we moved in. Not one damn roach."

"That makes sense. I bet the centipedes are eating the hell out of them in your walls, before they ever get to the inside of the apartment. I know Mr. Wong used to let a few of his run around the apartment and eat any of the roaches that came in."

Carl shook his head. "That dude was sick in the head. We were dreading life for a few days after we first saw this fucker and knew he was roaming around the apartment." Carl jabbed his finger at the baggy, wishing he could send flames from the tip, as he said 'fucker'.

"So, then, what's the plan, Carl?"

Carl looked down at Derek, lips pursed in concentration, as his brain flipped through various possibilities then settled on the one he felt was right.

"Well, that depends. Can I get y'all's help?"

"That depends, Carl. What do you have in mind and what's in it for us?"

Damn, he's a handful, Carl thought.

"Well, my plan is to take a sledgehammer to those walls then torch every one of those bastards and their young. We can fry them with our little makeshift flamethrowers. Jessica can stand by with a fire extinguisher and I'll pull the batteries on the smoke alarm ahead of time. So, you guys want to cook some giant centipedes or what?"

All the boys' eyes lit up and they nodded their heads vigorously … except Derek. He had a sly look on his face.

"On one condition," he said.

"Name it," Carl answered.

"We get to keep some of them for ourselves. I saw Mr. Wong fight them against other insects, spiders, even small snakes and lizards. It was cool as hell. I'd like to make some videos and put them on YouTube. That'd be badass." Derek smiled big and the other boys chimed in their agreement.

Carl shook his head, unable to understand the attraction but he was willing to agree to the demands if it secured their assistance.

"You got it." Carl extended his hand to Derek and he took it, sealing the deal with a shake and their personal honor.

"Alright, I'll go to the store and buy plenty of lighters and cans of hairspray, the ones I owe you and the ones for the job, as well as flashlights, a sledgehammer, and a good-sized fire extinguisher. Meet me at my place in two hours. I'll play some music, loud enough to drown out the hammer strikes while we work. Good to go?"

"You got it, Mr. C," Derek said.

"Mr., huh?" Carl cocked an eyebrow at him.

"You've earned my respect, and then some. It takes some serious balls to do something like this."

Derek smiled and Carl smiled back, feeling kind of cool at that moment as he turned to head for the store.

\*\*\*\*\*

Carl walked into the apartment, arms loaded down with the supplies, and pushed the door closed with a foot.

Jessica glanced up from the kitchen sink to greet him and stopped short, scrutinizing the items he was laying down on the couch and trying to figure out what use he intended for them.

"Ummm … Carl. What's all that for?"

Carl looked up with a proud smile and boyish anticipation covering his face.

"Extermination, baby! Extermination!" he exclaimed.

"Derek and the boys will be here soon to help us out," he further explained.

Jessica clearly looked confused while simultaneously giving him a look that demanded a full explanation. Carl gave her a quick run-down, explaining everything Derek had told him and what his plan was.

"So, your plan is to smash the walls in and burn all the centipedes you find, and I'm going to put out the fires? That about it?"

"You got it, hon! Exactly!" Carl snapped his fingers and pointed both index fingers at Jessica with his thumbs cocked back, two guns ready to fire. He was obviously proud of his plan.

"Have you lost your fucking mind?" Jessica asked him, her tone incredulous.

Carl looked like she had slapped him squarely, his face twisting up, her question a bitter pill of disrespect against all his arduous work.

"No," he said bluntly. "I have *not* lost my fucking mind. I'm going to take care of this. Did you not hear me that we probably have tens of those monsters, if not hundreds, crawling within our walls? You just want to stand by and do nothing? You telling me you're gonna sleep just fine tonight, knowing that those bastards are there, in our walls, and may well end up on our bed again? You're good with that, are you?"

Carl shut up and just stared at Jessica, with a stiff neck and eyes set like flint. He was not backing down on this one, at all.

Jessica considered his questions and realized she did *not* want to sleep in that apartment and she was *not* ok with their situation.

"Fuck," she spat. "Alright, dammit. Let's do it."

Carl smiled big, walked over, grabbed Jessica by her upper arms and squeezed her as he planted a big kiss on her lips. He let her go and gave her a little slap on one shoulder.

"Now you're talking, sidekick. Let's cook this pig."

Jessica was ready to say something about the 'sidekick' remark, but the doorbell rang, just then, right on time.

\*\*\*\*\*

Nine Inch Nails played loudly in the background as Derek, Ricky, and Rodney got their makeshift flamethrowers ready and flanked Carl, giving wide berth for him to freely swing the hammer and take out portions of the wall. Another of the boys, Danny, oversaw the flashlight and knelt, shining it where Carl said he was first going to make a hole. His initial target was the wall directly against the water heater. If they were going to find something, the best bet was there. It also seemed likely, to him, that the greatest concentration of the critters would be there, as well. It was warm and dark. No doubt.

It took about four swings to open a decent hole to see inside. Danny shined the bright light in there and cried out, shrinking away from what he saw.

"What is it?" Carl asked and took the flashlight to look for himself.

"A n ... nest, I think," Danny stuttered out.

Carl knelt and lowered his head to get a good look, gloved hands supporting his upper body. Even knowing what Danny thought, the sight of them still gave him a chill. They were all over the plywood floor around the water heater. The wood appeared to be rotten to a large degree, as well. Carl could make out individual ones, uncurling and beginning to move around due to the light and vibrations, while several giant centipede mothers curled more tightly around the masses of eggs they held between their many legs. But it was the few he spotted that had a mass of tiny newborn centipedes clutched within their circled bodies that got Carl. A shiver ran up his spine and caused his whole head and shoulders to shake briefly as if trying to throw off some instinctive, primal fear of such things.

"Fuck me," Carl mumbled, his worst nightmare come to life. He mentally told himself to cowboy-up and not let his fears control him. It took some internal struggle and deep breathing, but Carl managed to cast off the terror-stricken paralysis he felt.

"Alright. I'm gonna make a much bigger hole. Hopefully we can get to them without setting the whole place on fire. Be ready to stomp anything that comes out, though, while I'm clearing the plaster away."

The boys nodded in understanding. Danny looked a little nervous as Carl handed him the flashlight back.

Carl swung the hammer over and over in a quick secession of strikes, breaking the drywall and pulling it out of the way. Three of the giant centipedes came crawling out, startling Carl, and causing him to jump back, which made the boys flinch away and yelp. Carl lunged forward again without hesitation, swinging the sledgehammer down on one of the giant centipedes, smashing it right in the middle of its body. Derek and the boys trapped the other two with some of Jess's Tupperware to take in payment as their pets, while Danny shined the light on the hole to see if any more were coming.

Carl pulled the final piece of the wall back and held onto it, clearly exposing a good 4'x4' hole for the boys to work with.

"Oh, Fuck!" Danny exclaimed and pointed at Carl.

Carl had enough time to say "huh" and start to look around before the giant centipede cleared his glove and crawled up onto his forearm, clawed legs gripping his flesh. He flailed his arm hysterically, almost knocking Jess and the boys in the head as he spun in circles screaming 'fuck' repeatedly. He was able to see the length of it covering his forearm, the very rear legs locked onto his glove right before the centipede bit down on the crook of his elbow.

Carl screamed like a goat on fire.

His free hand cycled up and down rapidly, slapping at the creature in an unsophisticated flurry while shrieking like a baboon under attack. It had absolutely no effect. The giant centipede did not let go but bit him again and hung on with the poisonous mandibles and its numerous legs. Powerful jaws began gnawing into Carl's flesh with a single-minded purpose. His arm burned horribly from the venom. He might as well have torched his own arm, it wouldn't have hurt any worse.

"Pull it off, Mr. C!" Derek yelled. "Pull it off!"

Carl managed to hear and process Derek's words in the midst of his primitive panic and finally gripped the body of the centipede as close to the head as possible, then ripped back, pulling it off his arm, though some of his flesh came along with it. Carl squeezed as tightly as he possibly could, trying to crush the monstrous bastard, but he could not overwhelm its exoskeleton.

"Spray him down, Derek, along with my glove!"

Derek gave Carl a look that said, 'Are you sure?', and Carl immediately nodded. Derek hosed the centipede and the glove, thoroughly, as it thrashed about.

"Light it," said Carl.

"You got it, Mr. C," Derek responded, and flicked the lighter, sparking the flame that set Carl's whole hand on fire, along with the centipede.

Carl held his clenched fist up, for as long as he could, watching the flame-engulfed centipede crackle, before the hairspray burned off, and the glove, itself, began to catch on fire. He threw his assailant to the floor and stomped it a couple of times then shook the glove off and stomped it too, putting out the flames.

Carl stumbled over and collapsed on the recliner, a combination of curses, shouts and painful groans composing a repeating cycle of noises that erupted from his mouth for some time. It was excruciating agony. He had read about it. The venom wasn't poisonous, but it could put a grown man on his ass, crying like a wimpy little bitch for a few hours.

Carl didn't have time for that, though. He didn't have time for anything except killing these sons of bitches.

"Are you alright?" Jessica asked, genuinely concerned for him.

"Do I *fucking* look alright!?" he shouted. "*It fucking hurts like thirty hells!* Arrrgghhh!!

*Motherfucker*!!"

Carl's temper had climbed to a new peak. It wasn't directed at Jessica or any of the boys. It was aimed squarely at the centipedes and his piece-of-shit landlord, who wouldn't get an exterminator. It was his fault Carl was in pain. Of that, Carl was absolutely sure. Still, Jessica didn't appear to feel the difference, as her face showed the pain Carl's words had inflicted and she backed away from him.

It took Carl a few seconds to register what he had done.

"Baby, I'm sorry. I wasn't thinking. I'm just hurting like hell, and I reacted like an asshole. I'm sorry. Okay?"

They held eyes until Jessica believed he was serious and she softened.

"I forgive you," she said. "Do you want me to get something to bandage that with, and some triple-antibiotic ointment with the pain reliever in it?"

"Yes, please," he replied, "and about five extra strength acetaminophen."

He coughed and felt his lungs tighten, slightly. Carl knew he couldn't risk having a full-on attack right now. He retrieved the inhaler from his pocket and took a long hit off it. Then he stood and walked back over to the large hole in the wall, closely inspecting the portion he needed to hold out of the way for the boys. He pulled it back and used the sledgehammer to keep it from springing back to cover the hole.

Jessica returned and bandaged his arm up, wrapping everything from elbow to wrist with gauze, covering all the smaller scratches as well as the nastier bite marks. He downed the pain pills. Nothing was helping though. It was the most excruciating pain he had ever felt. Worse than the time he tore a rotator cuff muscle and couldn't move without stabbing pains that made him nauseous. Even now he felt his stomach flip flop and his mouth began to salivate.

"Don't puke," Carl muttered to himself as he retrieved the glove and slid it back on his left hand.

"OK fellas. Spray hairspray all over them along the bottom of the water heater first. Then hose the whole area with fire. It should burn them good while not immediately catching the wood on fire, I hope. Jess stand ready with that fire extinguisher."

Derek took point and coated the area with hairspray, watching the insects start to writhe around at the unfamiliar chemical. Then he flicked the lighter and let loose hell on the centipedes. The flames engulfed them entirely. Carl imagined he heard little screeches, but he didn't think it was likely he could have heard them over the music. Popping noises were quite audible, though, as the fire cooked them and their exoskeletons crackled. Their bodies flailed all about, the mothers trying to protect their roasting young, who died first. A few of the males came crawling out of the hole, burning like pieces of kindling soaked in kerosene. They ran for some distance, then began curling and contorting as they finally felt the full effect of the flames. The boys stomped them dead, putting out the flames simultaneously as well.

Carl let the fire burn for several seconds, monitoring it to make sure it wasn't getting beyond their ability to put out, but making sure it burned long enough to kill these gargantuan insects that had no place in this concrete jungle he called home.

"Alright, Jess. Let it rip."

Jessica stepped up and sprayed the interior of the hole thoroughly. She waited for the white powder to settle then inspected it closely, determining that the fire was out. She started to back up, then stepped forward again, spraying a little more for good measure.

Carl put on one of those ER masks and wrapped a T-shirt around his face to prevent him from breathing in the fire extinguisher powder.

"Light, Danny," he called, and Danny stepped up, handing the flashlight to Carl again. A lengthy inspection satisfied Carl that they had gotten everything he could see.

"All right. Moving on," Carl declared, picking up the hammer and shifting to another area of the wall.

Over the next couple of hours, he made smaller holes every few feet, and looked inside to see if there were any others. They spotted a few lone males scurrying around but no more females with eggs or babies. Derek got the bright idea to use a spaghetti spoon to reach in and drag the lone ones out into the open. They captured three more and burned the rest on the linoleum floor, melting it in multiple places.

By the end, Jessica and the boys were all hacking from the fire extinguisher powder and decided to put on masks and wrap T-shirts around their mouths to filter it out, just as Carl had done earlier. They went back and took a second look around the water heater. Finding nothing, Carl felt happy with himself and his plan. In the next few days, he would contact a friend who could help him with repairing the drywall, thereby keeping it off the landlord's radar.

Derek looked at Carl, with a smirk on his face.

"What?" Carl asked.

"Just thought of something. Made me laugh."

Carl gave him a look that said, 'spit it out, I know you're about to be a smartass'. Derek's smirk turned into a wicked grin.

"You know, you can totally expect to see roaches now, right?"

Carl dropped his head, and shook it back and forth, mumbling curses beneath his breath.

Derek just laughed.

*****

That night, Carl and Jessica lit the one lemon Yankee Candle they owned and set it in their bedroom to help mask all the nasty burnt wood and fire extinguisher chemical smells filling the apartment. Carl showered. Jessica slipped in to join him. They both breathed huge sighs of relief at finally being done with this nightmare. At first, they simply hugged each other for a long time, the hot water helping to burn away the disgust they both felt. After some time, they soaped one another down and enjoyed the feel of each other's flesh.

Once out, they toweled off, and Jessica dressed Carl's wound more thoroughly this time, cleansing everything with hydrogen peroxide before applying ointment. She then placed gauze pads over the deep bite marks and wrapped his whole arm with gauze and taped it down.

At last, all ready for bed, they crawled under the covers, unconsciously leaving the lights on. They snuggled up to one another and began kissing passionately. Jessica moved as if she was going to go down on Carl, but he checked her softly, his hand between her breasts, slowly pressing her to lay back and let him, instead. Pulling the sheet over his head, he disappeared. Carl showered her abdomen with butterfly kisses as he descended to caress the gates of paradise with his mouth.

Jessica groaned softly and made other soothing sounds of pleasure that dripped like a honey potion in Carl's ears, but soon grabbed his head and pulled upward.

"I want you inside me … now," she moaned and kissed him deeply. He entered her and began slowly cycling his hips, her own matching his movements.

Carl controlled each stroke, making sure Jessica's sensations built ever higher. It drove her crazy when he moved slowly like that. She loved it, but eventually, it caused her to desperately demand he give it to her with some authority and force.

"Harder!" she commanded him, breathless, and he obliged.

Three thrusts later Carl felt a sharp pain, right on the head of his penis. It caused him to pause unexpectedly. Jessica kicked his glutes with her feet as if spurring a horse on to run.

"Don't stop! Don't stop! I'm so close!"

Carl, despite the pain, continued, sacrificing his comfort to bring her to climax.

Another stabbing pain struck, and another, but he didn't stop. Jessica's whole body went rigid and she slowly raked the nails of both hands from spine to ribcage, leaving a trail of welling blood. If he had been in the moment, and not already in pain, Carl would have loved it, he thought, but, as it was, it just added to the discomfort he was already experiencing. As soon as Jessica shuddered and relaxed, he quickly pulled out, the pain on the head of his dick now in multiple places and not letting up.

He sat back on his haunches, pulling free of Jessica's arms and feet that were trying to keep him inside her. Then, he tossed the sheet back so he could get a clear look at his member.

"What's wrong?" she asked, sulking a little. But then, she saw his face and knew something was seriously wrong. Her stomach sank like a ship standing on end before sliding down into the murky depths beneath.

To his credit, Carl didn't freak out and scramble about with no sense of purpose. Instead, despite his face indicating a terrific degree of disgust, he sat still and pulled the small, milky white baby centipedes off the head of his cock, one at a time, then mashed their soft bodies in between thumb and forefinger before smearing them across the sheet to clear their filth off his hands. A total of three had attached themselves to him, whether by legs or bite he did not know. He only knew it hurt.

Jessica stared at him, confused, and, mercifully unable to connect the dots, at first. But when it finally hit her, she clawed violently at the manicured patch of hair above her vagina, digging toward the opening to pull her lips back, arching her hips up desperately like some whore pretending she must have the man who has paid her for a performance, her head straining, chin to chest, to give the eyes a better line of sight.

Right then, both Jessica and Carl observed a sight that would be burned into their minds for the rest of their lives.

*Baby centipedes are crawling out of my wife's pussy,* was all Carl could think as he watched them exit her vagina and spread out in various directions; scurrying down the inside of her thighs, up into the hair covering her pubic bone, and down onto the bed.

Jessica may as well have been an animal with its tail on fire at that moment.

She flip-flopped off the bed, slapping at her groin and clawing her thighs, screeching some inhuman noises the whole time. Carl could only compare her wretched uproar to that of abused animals in fits of absolute fear, who, when approached, cry out, over and over, pitiful and helpless.

Jessica was just like that, right up until Carl held her down, and removed every one of those little bastards he could find from her body.

Then he took her to the ER. Fuck the bill.

*****

**Two days later**.

Carl called in the favor from Derek, or at least he tried. Derek refused to charge Carl, instead volunteering his resources and aid. They wore gloves and masks, completely covering their faces when they broke into the rundown flat.

Derek was damn-near a master lock-picker at age twelve or thirteen. Carl still wasn't sure.

Nobody saw or heard them, except, perhaps, the crack addicts, who were high as a kite and not paying any attention at all. They slipped through the kitchen and down the hall to the bedroom. Carl was carrying a backpack and holding a cloth he had just soaked with ether, while Derek held some type of container.

The man on the bed snored loudly, then gasped as the air was forced from his lungs by Carl plopping down on his chest. He covered the man's mouth and nose with the cloth immediately. The man tried to struggle, but his obese and muscularly weak frame couldn't accomplish much before the ether won the day.

They moved quickly, removing long, heavy duty cargo straps from the backpack and proceeding to loop them over and under the bed, then ratchet them down tightly, restraining the man across the head, shoulders, waist, upper thighs, and knees. Once done, Carl took a pocket knife to the man's underwear, the only thing he was wearing, and ripped them off, exposing his genitals. Carl proceeded to nick the man's skin with the blade across the chest, inner thighs and even his flaccid penis.

Derek followed behind Carl, dropping a giant centipede on each location. They wasted no time biting into the bleeding flesh with their venomous pincers before beginning to chew their way inside.

Carl watched the one going to work on the man's shriveling member and remembered the pictures he had seen online of a fourteen-inch long giant centipede that ate its way into the mouth of a snake almost twice its size … then devoured it from the inside out, exiting somewhere near the tail.

After several seconds, Carl looked away and reached into the backpack for one last thing - an item used to keep a patient's mouth open during dental surgery. He pried the man's mouth open and shoved it into place.

*A fucking tunnel of love,* Carl thought, as he picked the last giant centipede up with the forceps, himself, and lowered it, letting it smell the man's fetid breath and feel the plastic edge of the device with its most front legs. It began to pull, its head descending into the warm, dark pit below. Carl slowly let go, watching the legs rise and fall in unison as the creature crawled into the landlord's mouth and began its trek down the throat.

The man startled awake, trying to cough as his eyelids flew wide open, double chin quivering, eyeballs straining to look in his own mouth.

Carl grinned with a sense of immense personal satisfaction.

"I told you what I'd do if another of those centipedes hurt my wife, fucker," Carl told the landlord then stuffed a rag down inside the oral device to muffle any screams and make sure the giant centipede couldn't crawl out.

*At least not through **that** hole, anyway,* he told himself, *"but it'll make **a** way out when it's ready.* The thought comforted Carl, scratching his vengeful desires behind the ears. His right leg damn near bounced in delight.

"Perfect," he said to Derek, a dark, menacing smile unseen beneath the mask.

"Warm, dark places are their favorite," Derek remarked callously.

Carl looked at where the other centipedes were clinging to the man's body, little powerful jaws cutting through his flesh as they burrowed inside. It was the closest thing to justice he could imagine.

"Let's go," he said to Derek.

They listened to the muffled gags and gurgling cries as they walked out the way they came in, making sure no one saw a thing.

*That's what you get for not hiring an exterminator and putting my wife through hell, you greedy, useless bastard,* Carl thought to himself.

They stayed in the shadows and moved in silence, eventually taking the masks off. They'd burn them tomorrow along with the gloves. The apartment complex came into sight. It was Carl who spoke first.

"Thank you so much, Derek. I know you wanted to keep those things."

"I've still got one, Mr. C. And one's all I need to fight against other bugs and stuff. I just wish I could get a look at that guy's body when they're done. Curious how much of him they'll eat before he gets found."

"You worry me, sometimes, Derek," Carl said flatly, cutting his eyes to give him a wink. "But I still think you're a good kid. Good to me and Jessica, that's for damn sure."

He patted Derek on the shoulders as they entered the building, then they parted ways, sharing a bond that no distance could ever break now.

# The End

# Afterward

Hi folks! If you have bought and read this little novella, I sing thee praises and extend my heartfelt gratitude unto you for taking a chance on me, a still budding Indie author. And now that you're done, I suppose I'll tell you exactly what motivated me to write this story, and what I really wanted to achieve.

As far as the driving impetus that made this story happen, over the last year or so, being involved in multiple horror groups for both movies and novels and following threads of various authors, a common theme that I hear people express is "Nothing really scares me anymore," "I can't find anything that scares me, I wish I could," or "I guess I'm just too desensitized, nothing bothers me."

Now, this annoys me on one hand, while on the other hand, I do understand the process of desensitization. If someone is watching and reading loads of extreme horror with all kinds of viscera on display and sick bastards doing ever more perverse and heinous acts to other people, after a while, one will become less affected by this type of thing.

At the same time, I think much of people's inability to be scared is that they have lost their ability to put themselves in the place of the characters who are suffering. They remain a spectator the entire time. The possibility that this could be them doesn't enter their mind, and so, there's never any real perceived threat to get under their skin, dig in their brain and linger on after the words or pictures have finished.

This is no good. Horror, whether visual or written media, should never be a spectator sport. Horror should be an immersive, consuming force of psychological nature, engaging primal fears in reflexive ways we are helpless to stop. Or, to use an old fantasy paradigm - the reader or viewer of horror should be "spellbound."

In writing 'Warm, Dark Places are Best' I strived to make it as experiential and plausible as possible. I wanted you to feel like this could be you and, hopefully, not give you a choice whether to be a spectator. I aimed to make Carl and Jessica's victimization vibrant and their emotions raw, and thereby make you feel like they were you.

Also, insects, in general, I realized, are part of most human beings inbred fears, and offer a straight shot to those unguarded, almost childlike, areas of the heart and mind that are still highly susceptible to being terrified more easily. But, beyond that, the idea of having most insects on our skin or in our hair, much less inside of us in the most vulnerable of places, is the epitome of the horrific.

And not only are centipedes one of the most terrifying, brutal, and ugly insects in the world, but the bastards are almost everywhere. Giant centipedes may only be native to jungles and certain desert climates, but internet shopping enables people to have them shipped right to their residences. So, they can, in fact, potentially be anywhere as well.

Now, as to my goal in writing this story. Obviously, from reading what I wrote above, I'm sure you can deduce that I wanted to scare and creep the shit out of you and hopefully make the "nothing scares me" people cringe and feel their skin crawl. And that is correct. But it went further. I specifically, at some point in this story (or possibly multiple places, if you're like some of my beta readers) wanted to make you throw (or sit) down whatever you were reading on and jump up and walk around cussing. Cussing me and the visual razor cuts my words just made in your brain that will certainly leave scars for life ... whenever they manage to heal.

I wanted you in shock and full of disbelief at the images I rudely inserted into your mind; replacing any sense of security in your daily life with a dreadful fear that might, for days, or even weeks, after, make your skin feel as if it's doing some maggot-infested dance, causing you to reflexively slap your body in various locations whenever clothing, or even your own hair, brushes up against you. Why? Because your brain will be swearing on a stack of bibles (in a panicked mental shriek) that it's a *fucking centipede*!!!

Which, by the way, I suggest looking up these legit little monsters online. Holy crap are these things brutal! Do a YouTube search like I did for "Giant Centipedes vs" and see what you get – lots of videos of people who have caught them in the wild or bought them online and now pit them against other insects, scorpions, small to medium-sized snakes, frogs, etc. just to see who will win.

The centipedes pretty much entangle the prey with all their legs and try to lock all their movement down, bite them with their poison filled mandibles which can paralyze most prey, and then they just start eating a friggin hole right through their victim. Doesn't matter where – midsection, skull, neck; it doesn't matter. They just chew through it. They're like the honey badgers of the insect world! Giant Centipedes don't *give a fuck*!

Hell, they'll even crawl right down the mouth of their victim and eat them from the inside out. I found a picture of where a 14" long giant centipede did that to a snake that was about two feet long. He was exiting near the tail when the picture was taken. Then they killed him and laid them both out next to a yardstick for another picture.

For two of the best and scariest pictures of giant centipedes I found, do the following. Google search "giant centipede Vietnam soldier." The first picture will be an old pic of a young soldier holding one up that is well over a foot long. Nasty. For the second picture, copy/paste the link in the footnote below.[1]

This is the best, and the clearest pic of a giant centipede I found anywhere, I think. It also gives the size of the centipede some nice perspective with the piece of wood it's stretched out on, plus a man's hand in the picture along with the mouse it is eating. Wickedly impressive, detailed and scary. (Shivers! UGH.) Moving on.

---

[1] https://www.pinterest.com/pin/328973947761767448/

Well, having read the story, you may be wondering why I would write this tale. Funny coincidence, because a few of my beta readers asked me, with what appeared to be an honest sense of sickened perplexity, "*Why*?!?!? *Why* would you *choose* to write about these things?" To which I initially answered, "Because something in my brain is squishy." ;)

But the honest answer is that this story was a true epiphany. I had the idea, plotted the basic story outline and wrote over 9,000 words all on the first day. I was in a major freakin' Zen Zone and the spice was flowing from some Bene Gesserit muse, to mix metaphors. I swear, I wouldn't have stopped at 1:00 am but I had to be up for work at six in the morning, so I made myself go to bed.

"From whence came this epiphany?" would be the natural question one might ask next.

Well, it's pretty much a three-fold answer.

First, about a week before the epiphany, I shared a video on Facebook where someone had gotten a centipede in their ear and had to have it removed. They used the water trick just like I did in the story. (In fact, I've seen another video on YouTube a year or so ago where they did the exact same thing to get a decent sized spider out of someone's ear.) People were freaking out, gagging, wanting to vomit, asking *why* I would share something like that and just all around extremely wigged out and disturbed by it. Which to any good police officer (or fairly observant critical thinking person) would be called a 'clue'.

Second, going back to my youth, I watched the first Creepshow movie when I was 9 or 10 and in the last story, there's an older man who ends up with an apartment infested with roaches. Eventually, they overwhelm him, eating their way inside his body. In the final scene, his body is laid out on a countertop. Suddenly, pinpricks of blood appear on his skin and show through his clothes. Then, without any further warning, hundreds, if not thousands, of roaches begin bursting out of this guy's body all over. I literally had nightmares for a month.

Now, before I reveal the third source of inspiration for my epiphany, indulge me and let me set the stage a bit.

I'm a tough guy. Not something I simply claim to be but something many people I have trained with and taught have said over the years.

I can fight. I have a heightened pain tolerance and can take a hell of a hit. In all my years of martial arts training, sparring and teaching (including being the bad guy and letting students hit me) as well as all the altercations I got in with criminals on the street as a cop, I have never been knocked out.

I voluntarily got shot with a Taser, and I stayed standing and ripped out the metal barbs.

I flew off an ATV several years ago at about 35 mph and hit face first in the side of a ditch bank – instant stop. I crawled out of the ditch and walked away from it, a little sore for a few days, but unharmed otherwise. My coworkers all said, "Dude … you're a fucking Neanderthal; if that had been one of us we'd have died or broken something."

When I had the total knee replacement surgery back in September, I got medical / scientific verification that my bones are far denser than the average person. According to my orthopedic surgeon my bone tissue is more tightly knit, and it took him twice as long to saw through my femur and tibia as it normally does.

In other words, at 6'4" 300 lbs. and able to move with the fast twitch hand speed of a lightweight in addition to all the other stuff above, I'm a bit of a freak of nature. I have friends who are probably more so than myself, but I think I squarely fit within the category based on my resume. And most people who know me or have seen what I can do empty handed or with a blade all swear they will shoot me or run me over with a vehicle if I ever come at them with ill intent.

I say all the above to draw this comparison - that despite all these badass traits, I am not a fan of certain insects.

I've always thought spiders were super cool … *somewhere over there.* (waves hands like shooing a child away). I love to look at them, watch them spin webs, catch prey and cocoon and sip on 'em, but I'll be damned if I want one touching me in *any* way *much less* crawling *on* me.

When I was 17 years old I wrecked my dad's Honda 3-Wheeler riding on the paths back in the woods on our property. There were these big round-bodied spiders that would spin webs that covered the entire path, which was wide enough for a pickup truck, and then sit right in the middle.

So, one day I'm running and gunning on the 3-Wheeler when suddenly, I felt this wispy crap hit my face and hair (long hair, I was a metal head and had hair past my shoulders back then). *ALL* I could think was that one of those big-ass, big-bellied spiders was in my long hair. I let go of the handlebars, immediately grabbed my hair and started slapping at my head. The wheel snapped sideways, and the bike started flipping.

I stayed connected, hugging it with my thighs, for about three rolls and then I let go. I tumbled about three more times on my own, popped up, and my legs gave out. I melted to the ground, still slapping my head and shoulders and checking my arms to make sure I didn't have one of those spiders on me. I walked away, pushing the ATV because it wouldn't start.

I also don't like hornets, wasps, or yellow jackets. Let one of them get too close, and you'll see my Kung Fu come out. In my younger days, I ran like a bat out of hell, but with the total knee replacement, not so much anymore.

Despite all this, like I said, I think spiders are cool. I even think wasps are badass critters. I find them all interesting. Except for roaches. Roaches are just nasty and disgusting. I hated walking in a rundown apartment or house, as a cop, that was full of roaches, especially when those bastards were on the ceiling and would drop down on you sometimes. Ugh! Nasty!

But worse than any other insects, are friggin' centipedes. I HATE centipedes. Even just the normal ones. Besides the fact that God made those bastards so vicious and ugly that by nature they tap into some primordial, instinctive fear inside us, He compounded the problem exponentially by enabling them to hide so damn easily.

I mean, think about it. When you see a spider, for example, you generally know exactly where that little sucker is going to be later on - in a web or within a particular little area. But frackin' centipedes will move from room to room in your house and are very hard to find.

Which brings me to the third part of my epiphany: my own personal experience with centipedes. How things start out going badly for our main characters in 'Warm, Dark Places are Best' is completely based off what happened to my wife and me several years ago. Carl waking up to one crawling on his shoulder, slapping it off and then being unable to find it? Yeah, happened two nights in a row to me. We were sleeping with the lights on, ear plugs and underwear. Luckily, I spotted the bastard in the kitchen, just like Carl, a few nights later and stomped his ass to death. Building on that, I just ratcheted up the level of violation to, apparently, based on my beta readers' feedback, some ungodly levels. (Innocent look)

All in all, I realized that by writing a story with these centipedes, I could tap into a very deep-rooted, instinctive fear that is common to most of mankind; and by making it plausible and potentially close to you at any time, even in your home, I have managed to evoke a loathsome and lingering paranoia in many of my beta readers (some of which are even avid extreme horror veterans).

And my hope is that I have done the same thing to you. (Sweet smile)

Now you can suffer with me, like when I was a child; waking up sweating, with visions of crawling things not only *on* me but *inside* me.

Well, they say shared traumatic experiences bring people closer, sooo … I think this might make us friends now if we weren't before. I sure hope so. :)

Printed in Great Britain
by Amazon